FADED FAMILY

JADE AYOMETZI-CUEBAS

FADED FAMILY

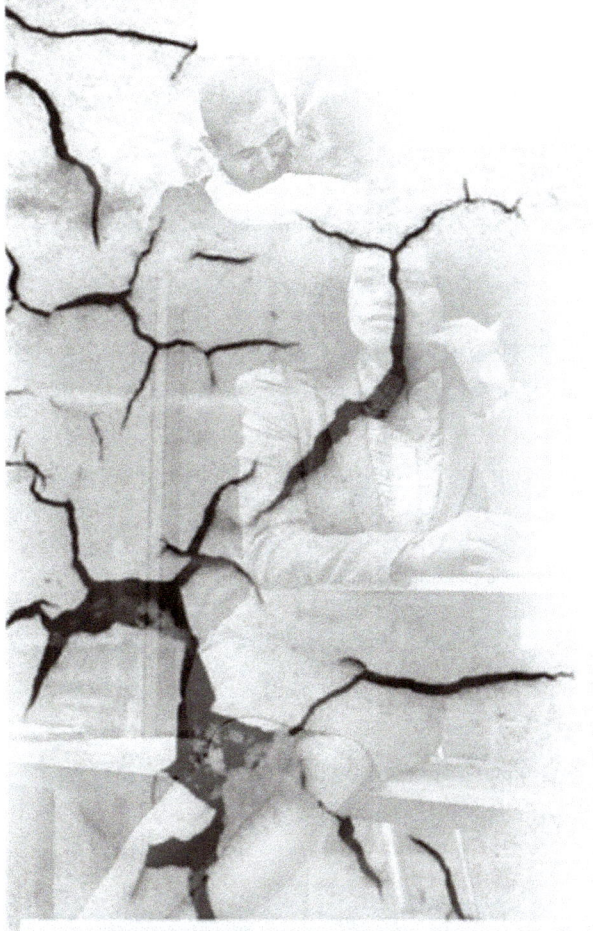

JADE AYOMETZI-CUEBAS

SBPC

SIMMS BOOKS PUBLISHING CORP.

Publishers Since 2012

Published By Simms Books Publishing Jonesboro, GA

Library of Congress Cataloging in Publication Data

2025937127

Jade Ayometzi-Cuebas

Faded Family

ISBN: 978-1-949433-65-4

Edited by A.J

Book Arrangement by Simms Books Publishing Corp.

Cover by: Jade Ayometzi-Cuebas

Dedication

I would love to thank my family, my brothers, and my parents, for always supporting me and my writing dreams. I would love to thank All my friends, teachers, and various therapists, who have supported me throughout all of my troubles.

It is because of you All I was able to write this.

Chapter 1

It was a typical day at Sona Corporations. Throughout the office, Arek had been distributing papers and other significant materials. When he arrived at the final office—Elena's workspace—he hesitated. She was one of the company's chief executive officers, an extremely significant individual; the organization might have collapsed entirely without her. He therefore knew better than to just walk in.

In addition to being polite, he knocked on her door to see if she was there.

"Come in!" a voice screamed, followed by the door creaking. Arek entered.

"I have the updated documents you asked for, Miss Elena," Arek said in a cool, stern tone.

"Good morning to you too," Elena replied in a jokey manner as Arek placed the papers on her desk.

As he was on his way out to return to his desk, Elena began to speak. "No, come, sit down."

She gestured for Arek to sit in a chair. Arek didn't want to. He wanted to keep working; otherwise, they'd both be at risk. But he would be at risk if he said yes or no, so his opinion didn't matter.

So Arek sighed and went back to his boss, sitting next to her and helping her fill out the documents, neglecting his own work. After about two hours, they finished the paperwork.

"Can I go now, Miss?"

"Please, Arek, you know my name. Use it," she said, smirking as her hand brushed against Arek's lap.

Arek seemed startled by the sudden affection but didn't entirely mind. One thing led to another, and after work, they made plans to meet up at Elena's house to continue their little work session.

Afterward, Arek woke up in the middle of the night. He quickly put on his clothes and drove away, not bothering to wake up Elena. He was just wondering what he had done. It didn't feel right, but not entirely wrong either.

Arek felt he was also at fault in some way, shape, or form. He hated the feeling in his gut, but he could not help it.

The morning hit, and Arek called in sick for work. He needed some time to think and clear his mind. But a day off work is still only a day off. So, he had to return the next day.

The next day, Arek tried everything in his power to avoid Elena. But avoiding her was practically impossible. Things kept happening between the two of them, but not to that extreme level again.

Elena took any chance she had, any break or opportunity to go see Arek. And Arek, while not being completely okay with it, didn't see it as totally wrong either.

That was until three months had passed.

It was just a regular Friday morning until Elena called Arek to her office. Arek got up from his desk and headed to her office. He knocked on the door, and Elena opened it.

"Do you need something, Ella?" Arek asked. It was his nickname for her. He used it sparingly, but he could just see she was stressed, and he felt it was right to use it to help calm her down.

"No. Um… here." She then handed him a pregnancy test. Arek looked at it and saw a tiny plus sign.

At that moment, he felt his heart stop for a bit. It felt like something had hit his gut with a swift punch.

"...You're pregnant?" he said quietly, his eyes widening as he looked at Elena's shameful expression. It was clear this was a massive mistake, and she knew it. She never intended for this to happen, and that much was clear.

She didn't want to be a mother.

Arek took a step back and seemed to be processing

4

it. This was a big deal, and if the company found out, they'd both be in trouble and possibly fired. Arek remained silent, as Elena looked down, devastated. Arek soon realized he had to make a decision.

"...After work, we'll head to the doctor for an appointment. You can make any decision you think is necessary. You can count on me, Ella; I'll always be here," he said, ready to take responsibility.

Elena lifted her head, smiled, and gave Arek a big hug. "Thanks, Arek...You're the best," she said through some tears.

It was emotional, yes, but it was clear they would work through it together...or at least, that's what he thought.

Chapter 2

The rest of the day, Elena and Arek were very close. Elena often joked about the soon-to-be baby. The other workers brushed her off as just making jokes about the topic, but Arek knew the truth.

Work was dismissed at 5:00 p.m. Arek waited outside the building.

Elena usually left work later than most other employees. Around an hour later, she made it, and off they went to the nearby clinic.

It was last-minute, so they waited.

And waited.

And waited.

When they were finally admitted, it was around 7:30 p.m.

The doctor, Dr. McCraw, asked them several questions and examined Elena, running some tests.

After about another half-hour, Dr. McCraw came back into the room. "Since it's too early, we can't tell the baby's gender, nor how healthy it is. It should be much more evident in a few weeks, so come back in about…four weeks. Just to make it clear, though so far, Miss Elena seems healthy, which is a good sign," he explained.

Arek felt a huge wave of relief hit him—Elena was healthy. But Elena seemed distraught, as if something was eating her up.

To make her feel more at ease, he took her hand into his.

"If that is all, you may go, and we will send your bill through the insurance, Miss Elena," Dr. McCraw said as he flipped through his papers and soon left.

Elena's eyes seemed so dull, almost lifeless. Arek couldn't help but feel bad, like this was his fault.

If he had only said no to her affection, this wouldn't have happened. And things could have been normal.

Arek, meanwhile, was ready to accept that he'd soon be a father. There was no doubt the child was his. So, he couldn't just escape the responsibility.

Things seemed drab for both of them, as their lives would soon change, but…maybe there was hope.

"Wanna go to Felix's Pizza place? We deserve some nice pizza," Arek said as they grabbed their belongings and exited the room.

Elena looked up, her eyes dilating a bit. "Sure," she said. And soon they left. And soon they were out on a nice… "Date." You could say. They ordered a good ol' pepperoni pizza, some lemonade, and a Coke. It was nice, in all honesty. It was a good distraction from their soon-to-be child.

They talked about work and other stuff, like their families and friends. But, soon, anxiety came back, striking Arek as he thought about the child. Would it be a boy or a girl, name options, and how their colleague, friends, and family would react?

Arek never wanted children either, he preferred to focus on his work. And so did Elena, but this child could stop that. As he wanted at least one parent to be a part of this kid's life.

After a long wait, Arek decided to bring the child back into the conversation. Almost killing Elena's happy mood. And it replaced with a disdainful look.

"We…We have to talk about the child, Ella. We can't hide the fact that you're going to give birth eventually. People will notice. People will ask questions! We have to be prepared-" Arek tried to explain in such a rush.

But Elena stopped him mid-sentence. "I know. Ugh, why must a stupid child cause so much drama for their parents?" Her voice was laced with hints of venom. It was clear what she thought of the child.

"Elena, you know an abortion isn't an option. There are no places in our area close by that allow that service. So, abortion is not an option for us."

Arek tried to explain, but Elena just rolled her eyes in annoyance. But she still replied, but with clear disdain. Arek was gonna have to change her view on the kid…That would be hard.

Chapter 3

A few weeks went by, and so far, Arek and Elena had made the agreement that only their parents would know and the boss above Elena. That way drama would be limited. They also agreed to not have a marriage till they settled, and figure out the housing situation.

It seemed reasonable to them, so they went with it.

They also had found out about the child's gender; they would have a female baby. Arek seemed hopeful this news would cheer Elena up.

It did not.

Elena kept getting angrier, especially when her belly grew. She became self-conscious of what this baby would do to her body.

Arek would try to help soothe her concerns but Elena was a stubborn woman...A bit too stubborn.

Arek tried everything he could to make her feel better.

But nothing was working.

And then, almost like a flash. The nine months hit. Just like that. And Elena was in labor. After several long painful hours, Elena had delivered a healthy baby girl. Arek was there and he immediately held the baby in his arms, she was smiling and making noises. But the blissfulness was soon cut off by Elena, her glares digging holes into the poor child.

"So, what shall we name it?" She asked.

Arek was a bit taken out of it by her tone but brushed it off. "Well…I like Christina." He said, looking at his baby's pure little smile.

"Okay, Christina it is, her middle name can be Taylor," Elena said her tone softening as she saw how happy the phrase made Arek.

Even if she didn't care, she at least wanted to pretend she did.

"Great, wait, what about the last name?"

"She can have yours; my parents already disapprove." Elena interrupted.

Arek was perplexed as the names were something they pushed off for a long while. And Elena, well she was surprisingly cooperative.

The names were settled, and the baby.

Christina Taylor Dean.

A beautiful newborn.

Elena, meanwhile; was made to wait in the hospital for roughly a few weeks. But when they returned, Elena took a few days off of work, while Arek kept working. Brushing off anybody who questioned where Ms. Elena was.

After about a month of missing work, Elena sent a text to Arek.

-Hey, can we talk at your place?

-Sure

Arek felt some butterflies in his stomach, but it wasn't the good fluttery kind. It was more of the

…Terror filled blood-sucking kind.

As if this was bad.

But he ignored them. Like, let's be real. Elena wouldn't do anything to harm him…

Right?

Arek quickly left work and raced to his apartment where he saw Elena waiting near the door.

"Ella! Hey," he said, trying to put up an energetic front.

But his butterflies remained. "Hey…" She said, clearly less energetic than her little boy toy.

"So, whatcha wanna talk about?" He asked, faking a smile. His gut was yelling at him to run.

"I…Can't take care of Christina. I just can't, I don't like kids! - And I don't want her! And I might even be fired for this…I'm sorry Arek, I really am. But…You're…Fired. Here's your last check" she said and handed him a crumpled envelope. And booked it out of there as fast as possible.

When the realization hit Arek.

Ooh boy. It hit him like a bus.

"WAIT- BUT- WHAT DO YOU MEAN?"

He screamed but Elena already had left the complex.

Arek was shocked, he wanted to go and chase her down.

But his body was frozen shut. He heard her car engine start loud but slowly became more distant.

He remained silent. Their eyes wide opened as he looked down at the baby, who was peacefully sleeping in her little carrier. Arek silently picked it up.

Unlocked his door.

And went inside his house. Setting the carrier on his dining table.

He looked at the child one last time before he felt tears streaming down his face…

Chapter 4

The tears didn't fade. Rather they grew.

The emotions were hitting Arek all at once, and he felt close to a panic attack. He needed to support not only himself, but his child, and now with no job.

Arek's cries caused the baby, Christina, to wake up.

She saw her father crying, and reached out to him, spouting out nothing but baby gibberish. Arek hadn't noticed, too consumed by his thoughts.

When he suddenly heard some babbles and other nonsensical words. He sniffed and turned to the baby.

He walked over and picked her up, cradling her in his numb arms. The baby giggled, as Arek tried to smile. Trying to find joy in this small moment…But he just couldn't, his anxiety was eating him up. And he saw little to no way out. So, he went to the phone and called up his sister.

When she answered, he told her everything, it sounded like a total mess from the other side. His sister, Annie, told him that she'd be there shortly.

She lived roughly twenty minutes away. When she finally arrived, she saw her older brother crying on the couch while holding the baby in his arms.

Annie didn't say a word and just walked over and put her hand on her older brother's shoulder, as a way of comfort. Arek sniffled as he wiped some tears with his sleeve. He turned his head to Annie and felt his tears starting to build up once again.

Annie though had a way to make him stop, it was like her superpower. She always managed to change his mood, even with a simple smile. Maybe that's part of the reason he chose to call her and not their parents.

After around ten minutes, Arek had fully calmed his tears down. Mentally though, he was still a wreck. Annie tried to get Arek to retell her the story.

"So, what exactly happened?" She asked in a calm, soothing tone.

Arek looked at her once again with defeated tired eyes. "Elena…She fired me cause of Christina…Our baby" He replied, before adding. "I don't know what to do, I can't take care of a child by myself! I just can't, and now I don't even have a job!" He said as his breathing quickened; it was clear he was spiraling.

Annie looked at him with a sympathetic look, but then she took a glance at the baby. And her look of sympathy turned into a soft smile. "Ya know, it might not even be that bad. How about this, I'll lend you the money to pay your bills and buy stuff for the child, until you get a job again and can stabilize a living. After that, I'd be glad to watch Christina." She said, smiling brightly.

Arek's eyes shot wide open, and he seemed ready to cry again. "No, no, it's fine. You don't have to."

"But I want to." She interrupted him, before adding. "Besides, what else is family for?"

That was really the line that broke Arek, as the tears started to fall. This time from the gratefulness he felt. "Thank you. Thank you so much." He said as he wiped another tear away.

Annie just smiled back, she was willing to do it for her brother, for free too.

"Yeah, just promise me to always do your best raising Christina" She explained, and he nodded immediately.

After they discussed the arrangement, Annie had to leave.

Leaving Arek and Christina alone.

Arek took a glance at his daughter and smiled before cuddling her.

Chapter 5

A few months went by, and the arrangement was working well, even if Arek didn't have a job, he was stabilized thanks to his sister. Arek used all the money he was given for his daughter; she was growing up quickly too. Even her hair was starting to grow as well.

Things went well, even if it was stressful. Arek felt as if his daughter mattered more than anything else in his life.

His love was pure.

Unlike Ella's.

One day, Arek was playing with Christina when he got a call. He thought it was his sister, so answered. But it was a workplace he interviewed at.

When he got the call, he jumped up from happiness. Christina jumped up as well after seeing her dad do it.

Before she fell down because she was still just a toddler. Arek chuckled before he dialed his sister, to tell her the great news.

"Hello?"

"ANNIE GUESS WHAT!" Arek said practically yelling.

"Oh, what? Come on, tell me!"

"Ya know that job I interviewed for? The real estate one? They accepted me!"

"Really?! That's amazing! I'm so proud of you! I'll send you the money for this month, but that job does pay well. But again, if you need any help, I'll be more than glad to lend it."

"That's okay!"

Arek was smiling very wide as he spoke to his sister. He couldn't believe this was real. He finally got a job again, after months of searching! He glanced at Christina and smiled.

Chapter 6

2 years have passed since Arek became a real estate agent. And he was doing great.

His sister stopped sending him money, but he was okay with that. As he was doing just fine with his new salary.

He even had time to spoil his daughter occasionally when he wasn't working.

Like with a trip to her favorite play place or buying her some new toys.

Life seemed to finally be getting better for Arek.

And in the meantime, he and his sister became closer, this whole experience just might have been for the better in some aspects. After another few months, it was Christina's birthday. She was now three years old.

"Do you want anything, Christina?" Arek asked as

he hosted a small party with a few relatives.

Christina thought as she ate her cake. "I want Daddy to play with me!" She said sweetly. Arek smiled and bent down to her level.

"How about tomorrow I take the day off and we can spend the whole day together?"

That sentence brought a big smile to Christina, as she squealed and gave her cake to her auntie and hugged her father.

Arek hugged her back and said so many sweet things to her. Saying how she was his everything. It made Christina giggle, as she thought they were nice. Not knowing the true impact, the words meant.

Another year had gone by in a blur. And Christina was now in kindergarten. She had started school, giving her father more time to work in peace.

More years went by, and Christina's personality grew from a sweet, innocent baby to a nice, smart, and well-adjusted kid. She had an interest in basketball. So Arek saved up enough money to sign her up to a kiddy team.

Everything was going swimmingly. And Arek had nothing but great thanks to his daughter.

Even if he got stressed, he wanted Christina to have one loving parent.

But as she grew up, entering sixth grade next month. She started to question where was her mom.

She used to ask when she was little, but it was only now she realized that her mother probably left. And Arek hated talking about her.

It was the one thing that turned him visibly mad. The only time the sweet girl, Christina has ever, EVER, seen him mad.

Christina, on the fateful day, was watching TV, while her father worked. When suddenly, there was a knock at the door.

Chapter 7

Christina was closer, and not really busy so she got up and answered it. Before she saw a woman, a woman she never saw before. Maybe it was one of Aunt Annie's friends.

"Hello Christina, is your father home?" The strange lady asked.

Christina was a bit perplexed by how she knew her name. But nodded. "Yes, he is. Why?"

"I need to talk to him." The strange lady said.

Christina was suspicious but, again shrugged it off. "Okay, Dad, someone's here to see you!" Christina yelled, catching her father's attention.

He ran from his study to the main room, and when he saw the lady, his body froze.

It was her.

"Elena…" He said quietly as a mouse. Christina

was confused, her dad knew this lady?

"Hi Arek, I know I have a lot to make up. But I need you, the company has been struggling recently. And I thought maybe you'd wanna come back to us?" She asked, pleading with him.

"Are... Are you serious? After everything you've done?!" Arek screamed at her, his body was overwhelmed by everything he's been through thanks to her.

Christina was still there, behind her dad. And she looked at the strange lady. Who looked back at her.

"Hey..." Elena said, Christina waved hello back to her.

Arek meanwhile grew angry.

How dare she come back for his help when she was the reason he struggled? Suddenly in an angered tone, he screamed at Elena.

"My daughter doesn't talk to strangers!" He then pushed her out of the way and slammed the door.

Christina was shocked to see so much anger from her dad. He got angry sometimes of course, but never to the point of yelling and pushing someone. And especially not slamming the door in their face.

Christina took a look at her dad, "Dad. Who was she?" She asked, her voice laced with confusion.

Arek turned to her and felt his anger melting away. "No one… Go watch TV, and don't let that woman ever come near you again." Arek said strictly, Christina nodded.

"Good…Christina, you're my everything. And I promise to never leave you." He said and gave Christina a big hug.

Christina was puzzled by this, but that was because she was a child. Soon she'd understand everything, and when that time comes. She'll have her parents to thank.

Author's Note

Hi everyone!

Hope you enjoyed my second book ever!

My first book is called "Painted Petals" and currently resides in Hampton High School Library.

I hope to write more in the future and inspire other kid writers such as myself. Remember you can do anything that you put your mind to, stay focused and love what you do it can happen!

I hope you enjoyed it as much as I had fun making it! BYE!

www.ingramcontent.com/pod-product-compliance
Lightning Source LLC
Chambersburg PA
CBHW070812120626
46557CB00002B/824